☑ The
☑ Wish
☑ List
☑ Della Galton

soundhaven books

Published 2014, in Great Britain, by
soundhaven books
(soundhaven.com limited)

Text Copyright © Della Galton 2014

All rights reserved. No part of this publication may be reproduced, stored in a retrieval system, or transmitted in any form or by any means, electronic, mechanical, photocopy, recording or otherwise, without prior written permission of the copyright owner. Nor can it be circulated in any form of binding or cover other than that in which it is published and without similar condition including this condition being imposed on a subsequent purchaser.

Please visit
www.soundhaven.com
for contact details

ISBN: 978-1500294625

British Cataloguing Publication data:
A catalogue record of this book is available from the British Library

Published by Woman's Weekly as
'The Wish List'
June 2003

This book is also available as an ebook.

About Della Galton

Della Galton is a novelist, short story writer and journalist. She's had over a thousand short stories published in the UK alone and she's run out of fingers to count her books on.

She is a popular speaker at writing conventions and the agony aunt for Writers' Forum Magazine.

When she is not writing she enjoys walking her dogs around the beautiful Dorset countryside and beaches.

Find out more about Della Galton, her books, speaking engagements & workshops, on her website, dellagalton.co.uk

*For Peter
who made me believe it is possible to find
your soul mate
with much love
Della*

The Wish List

☑ Chapter One

As I passed the landing window I saw Annette's Mercedes pull into my drive. She was late. Annette was always late, but she was my best and oldest friend and I couldn't think of anyone I'd rather celebrate my divorce with. I went downstairs to let her in and she breezed through the hallway and into my kitchen, smelling of fresh air and the light, flowery scent she always wore.

"Hi, Wendy. I thought you might have drunk all the bubbly by now so I've brought some more." She clunked the bottle onto the table, shrugged off her coat and hung it on the back of a kitchen chair.

"Don't leave it there." My voice was sharper than I'd intended, and she glanced at me, eyebrows raised.

"Sorry," I said. "Old habits die hard. I might have got my Decree Absolute, but life without Robert is going to take a bit of getting used to."

"You can say that again." Her green eyes were warm. Then she held out her arms.

"Congratulations. Give me a hug. I'm as delighted as you are. Well, very nearly!"

We hugged and when we pulled apart she glanced at her coat, still on the chair, and said, "Is that where you put your coat at home, Annette?" in such a perfect imitation of Robert's voice that goose bumps went up my arms.

"Don't. It still hasn't sunk in that he's never going to come walking in here again."

"Strutting," she corrected. "I never saw Robert walk anywhere, he always strutted." She did a pretty passable impression of my ex, up and down the kitchen, throwing her shoulders back and sticking out her chin.

"Stop it. I want to forget about him."

"But at least you're smiling now. So, come on, pour us some champagne. Or would you rather go out and celebrate?"

"No, I want to stay in and make a mess."

She giggled. "Sounds good to me. Where shall we start?"

Three quarters of an hour later we were in the lounge, me sitting on the rug on the floor, and Annette with her legs curled on the chair and her shoes discarded carelessly on the soft, white carpet. Between us, on the coffee table, stood a half empty bottle of Moet, a completely empty chocolate box and a big bowl of pistachios. Shells littered the glass tabletop.

"I feel quite light headed," Annette said, glancing round the room. "Although I can't decide whether it's the shock of being in here and knowing Robert isn't going to barge in and tell us off for making a mess, or the champagne. I think we need something more substantial than nuts and chocolates to soak it up. Have you got any decent pizzas in your freezer? Or are you on a diet?"

I glanced at the coffee table. "I think I've already blown it for tonight."

In the kitchen I hummed as I rummaged in the freezer, which I'd bought and filled up the previous month. It was the first one I'd ever had because Robert hadn't liked them. Everything had to be fresh. All his meals cooked from scratch. In a gesture of defiance, I'd picked out the biggest, shiniest freezer I could find, but there'd still been a shakiness in my stomach, which had transferred itself to my fingers as I'd written out the cheque.

As I put the pizza onto a baking tray it slid through my hands, frisbeed across the work surface and crashed into the toaster. *Butter fingers*, said Robert's voice in my head. I'd thought that divorcing him would be the most difficult part, but it was just beginning to hit me that it wasn't as straightforward as that.

I couldn't go back to being the old Wendy Mason. I'd been naive and idealistic when I'd joined Robert's practice as a trainee dental nurse. He'd had a reputation for being short tempered. Not the type to suffer fools gladly, but that hadn't bothered me then. Robert may have been pickier than the other dentists, but he was also a lot better looking. And he was the boss, so he was entitled to be picky. A smile or a word of praise from him was worth much more than from anyone else. I didn't notice that as time went on it got harder to please him, not easier, but perhaps that was because by the end of my first six months I was already in love.

I sighed as I adjusted the dial on the oven. The only link I had with the girl I'd been back then was Annette. We'd been best friends at school despite the fact that we couldn't have been more different. Annette was extrovert, clear headed and sure of herself. When I'd gone to work for Robert, she'd joined the family business as a sales rep. Her father owned a chain of animal feed outlets. At around the same time that I'd married and given up work, Annette's father had died and left her the business.

She was the only friend I had who hadn't drifted off across the years. None of my friends had felt that easy around Robert, but he'd never fazed Annette. Not much ever did faze her. She'd had plenty of boyfriends, but she'd never married. "It's far more fun being single," she said frequently. She was too supportive a friend to criticise my choices though. Although I knew she and Robert didn't see eye to eye, I hadn't even realised how much she'd disliked him until I'd told her we were getting divorced.

I took knives and forks into the lounge and we finished the champagne and opened the other bottle while we waited for the pizza.

"So, have you decided what you're going to do with your divorce settlement?" Annette asked. "Buy a new car, redecorate the house, or do you fancy coming on a Caribbean cruise with me?"

"None of those."

"But you've got to do something to mark the occasion."

"There are lots of things I fancy doing. I'm just not sure where to start."

"Maybe we should make a list."

I smiled. "Funny you should mention that." I got a piece of paper from my pocket and handed it to her. "I found this when I was clearing out the last of Robert's stuff. I wrote it years ago. It's a list of things I wanted to do before I was forty. It may sound silly, but finding it now feels like a bit of an omen."

Annette looked interested. She put her glasses on and started to read aloud.

"Number one, jump off the top board of the swimming baths." She glanced at me. "You must have done that, surely?"

"I'm scared of heights," I reminded her. "Not to mention being the most accident prone person in the universe."

"Most of that was down to Robert's sniping," Annette said briskly, and carried on reading.

"Number two, learn to belly dance, number three, cuddle a newborn piglet." She smiled. "Number four, spend a night outside, Number five, save someone's life. Number six, go skinny-dipping. Number seven, fly a plane. Blimey, that's a tricky one. Number eight, dye your hair pink. Number nine, shoe a horse." She shook her head. "That's a strange thing to want to do. I like number ten, though. I've always fancied doing that myself."

"I'd have thought you'd have done it hundreds of times."

"You'd be surprised." She studied me thoughtfully. "It's three weeks until your fortieth, isn't it?"

I nodded.

"So, why don't you start with doing the things on this list?"

"I don't think I was being particularly serious when I wrote it."

"But that's all the more reason to do it, surely." She put the list on the table. "You've spent the last fifteen years taking things too seriously. Thanks to Robert."

My face must have still been doubtful, because she grinned encouragingly and poured us both another glass of champagne. "Oh, come on, Wendy. Let's do it. This could be fun."

Chapter Two

Fun wasn't the first word that sprung to mind as I stood shivering in the changing rooms of our local pool the following morning. I felt hung over, underdressed and rather silly. I told Annette all this as we put our clothes in our lockers, but she wasn't impressed.

"You'd never forgive me if I let you back out now," she said, pulling her towel tighter around her with one hand and giving me a little shove across the changing room, with the other, "Anyway, we're here, so we might as well go and at least look at the diving board."

I went reluctantly ahead of her. It was years since I'd been in our local swimming baths, but it hadn't changed much. It still had pale blue walls, smelt strongly of chlorine, and was, at the moment, packed with children.

"Perhaps Saturday morning wasn't the best time to come?" I hedged.

"We won't be here long." She raised her eyebrows. "Five minutes at the outside and then we can sort out your belly dancing lessons."

"All right." I headed towards the dive pool, which was separate from the main swimming pool. "I think they've added an extra board," I told Annette. "I'm sure it never used to be as high as that. Maybe the second one down would be better."

"Oh, don't be such a wimp. It can't be that scary, or all those kids wouldn't be doing it."

As she spoke, one of them flew through the air in a graceful arc and hit the water with barely a splash.

"See, it's easy."

I didn't bother to answer this. We'd reached the steps and she went ahead of me. "I'll come up and give you some moral support," she said.

As we climbed, another child flew past us, hit the water with a resounding slap and came up crying.

"It serves you right," called out an unsympathetic sibling from the side of the pool. I told you it was too high. You need to build up slowly."

I glanced at Annette.

"Oh, just get on with it," she said.

There was a queue for the top board and I couldn't help noticing that no one in it was over the age of ten. I joined the end, clamped my teeth together to stop them chattering, and decided that I must have been drunker than I'd thought last night to agree to this.

The queue was going down at an alarming rate. There were three kids ahead of me, then two, then one: a little girl with blond pigtails.

"You can go first if you like," she said generously. "I've got cramp in my foot."

I knew how she felt. Only my cramp was in my stomach, which was twisting alarmingly and I wasn't anywhere near the edge yet.

"It'll end in tears, Wendy, you know how accident prone you are. Why don't you ever think things through?" Robert's voice was so clear in my mind that I cast a swift, anxious glance over my shoulder. Annette gave me an encouraging, 'you can do it', grin and I thought about what she'd said last night.

"He's done a demolition job on your confidence, Wendy, that's the trouble. It's going to take time to build it up again. It won't happen overnight."

She was right there. I clung onto the cold metal of the ladder we'd just come up and took a deep breath. I couldn't back out now because this wasn't just about jumping off a diving board, this was about – I struggled to remember what exactly it was about. It had made so much sense last night in my lounge.

Beside me, Miss Pigtails was standing on one foot while she massaged the toes of the other.

Stalling for time, I said, "What's the – er – best way to do this then?"

"It's easy. You just jump. But make sure you jump away from the end, or you might bash yourself going down."

"Right."

"You'd better take your towel off too," she called as I edged past her.

I bundled it up and threw it at Annette, who was smiling encouragingly from a safe distance.

"Don't look down," Miss Pigtails shouted, obviously getting into the swing of things now. "Or you'll make yourself feel sick."

I already felt sick. A mixture of fear and last night's overindulgence. The board trembled, as I stepped onto it. It wasn't the only one.

"And try not to do a belly flop 'cause it doesn't half hurt." I think someone else shouted that out, but I couldn't be sure. I took another tentative step. Perhaps I wouldn't go right to the end.

"You can do it." A chorus of voices came from behind me. Where had they all come from?

"Wendy, don't forget to hold…"

But whatever pearl of wisdom Annette was about to impart came too late, because before I got any further, I felt myself overbalancing and falling. And the water was coming up to meet me way too fast. Smack. I'm not sure which bit of me hit it first; suffice to say that it wasn't the most graceful of descents and there was considerably more than a small splash.

Fortunately, I'd remembered to shut my mouth and hold my breath. That must have been what Annette had shouted, I thought as the water closed over my head. When I resurfaced I could hear cheering. But all I felt was an enormous sense of relief. I'd done it and I was still in one piece. It took a few seconds longer to realise that my swimming attire was not. The top half of my bikini had somehow come unclipped on impact and was floating on the water about three feet away.

Blushing furiously, I made a grab for it, hoping that no one had noticed, but as my fingers closed around it and an even louder cheer went up from the top diving board, my hopes were dashed.

"You could have told me," I fumed at Annette, a few minutes later, when, bikini top safely in place once more, I climbed out of the pool. But Annette was laughing far too much to speak. And when she did manage to contain herself, all she said was, "I wish I'd bought my camera. You should have seen the expression on your face when you fell off that board."

I glared at her and she added, "Anyway, I think you'd better do it again. It definitely says jump on your list. I'm not sure falling off counts."

After a reviving cup of tea in the pool canteen, and two big pieces of chocolate gateaux, which I made Annette pay for to make up for laughing at me, I was beginning to see the funny side myself. Rather to my surprise I was also on a bit of an adrenaline high. The Wendy who'd been married to Robert would never have done anything so silly. Nor would the girl who'd gone into the freezer shop last month. It was strangely liberating.

"What are you thinking?" Annette asked.

"Nothing."

"Look on the bright side," she said. "You can cross off the skinny dipping bit now too, and everything else on your list is going to be a breeze in comparison to that."

"Famous last words," I said.

☑ Chapter Three

When we phoned up about belly dancing lessons, we were told that the next seven-week course didn't start for a month, so that was out. Secretly, I was rather relieved. I was sure that belly dancing would require all sorts of co-ordination skills that I didn't have.

"Cuddling a newborn piglet's easy," Annette said. "One of my customers is a pig farmer. His name's Patrick. He's quite tasty, actually."

"Patrick, the pig farmer?" I raised my eyebrows. "I don't think so."

"I wasn't trying to matchmake." Annette shot me a look. "Give me some credit. "He's got horses as well. So maybe, we could organize the shoeing bit with him too."

"I'm not sure that this was such a good idea," I said. "A Caribbean cruise would be a lot safer."

"Oh, but that would be soooo boring." She grinned at me. "Come on, Wendy, I'm enjoying myself."

In the end I gave in and agreed that she could arrange things. At least I wouldn't have a hangover on our farm trip. How bad could it be?

The Wish List

My visions of a picturesque farmhouse set in rolling green acres were shattered when we arrived at Home Farm at ten o'clock the following Thursday. We parked in a potholed lane outside a dingy house. Then we picked our way past various bits of rusting farm equipment that were lying about the front garden, and rang the doorbell.

Patrick turned out to be a dead ringer for the farmer on the Vicar of Dibley, tall and dark, with serious eyes. He was wearing a grubby looking blue boiler suit.

"You want to cuddle a what?" he said to Annette, his eyebrows meeting in a caterpillar frown on his forehead.

"A piglet. Remember? I mentioned it on Tuesday." She smiled sweetly at him. "You must have a few about the place. A quick cuddle and we'll be off."

Patrick blinked at her as if he was having trouble taking this in and I couldn't say I blamed him.

"It really doesn't matter," I said. "It was a silly idea. Forget we came."

"No – no it's fine." He smiled then and shook his head. His expression had evolved from faint bafflement into one of benign amusement. An adult humouring two rather silly children. "You'd better come in. I'll see what I can do."

He led us into a huge old kitchen that was dominated by an ancient black stove, which had something foul smelling simmering on one of its rings. A huge pile of washing up towered in the sink. In the middle of the kitchen, two collies thumped their tails, but didn't move from their position by the stove.

"What's that disgusting smell?" Annette wrinkled up her nose.

"Offal for the dogs." Patrick led us through a back door into a courtyard. "Over there. Help yourself." He pointed to a barn across the way. "Doris won't mind – but don't try taking them out of her sight."

"Doris," I muttered, glancing at Annette.

She nodded, sagely. "Mummy Pig." But I think even she was a little wary of what we were going to find as she opened the door. We went into a dimly lit barn, which smelt a great deal better than Patrick's kitchen. There were some hay bales piled in one corner and the floor was neatly swept. "He obviously spends more time out here than he does inside," Annette murmured.

The Wish List

We found Doris stretched out in a pen with at least fifteen piglets attached to her. Her eyes were closed and every so often she shifted and gave a soft sigh and one of the piglets would lose its grip and squeal and snuffle a bit, until it got back in position.

"Well, go on then," Annette said.

"I can't just pull one off."

"Course you can. Doris won't mind. Patrick said, didn't he? Just don't run off with it."

I bent over the pen. There was something very calming about the scene in front of me. The pen was spotlessly clean, the piglets pink and healthy looking. It was somehow not at all what I'd expected.

"Hi, Doris. Mind if I borrow one of your babies?"

Doris didn't stir. She didn't even glance in our direction.

One of the piglets came up for air and I gently scooped him up. He was warm and smooth and unbelievably cute. He snuffled against my fingers and squeaked a bit.

"Ahh," Annette said. "I wonder how old they are."

"Three days old," Patrick said, coming in behind us and looking into the pen with an expression resembling paternal pride. "I'm just about to make some elevenses if you fancy joining me?"

I glanced at Annette. I wasn't too sure about eating anything in Patrick's kitchen, but it would have seemed rude to refuse. Anyway, there was a warm wetness on my fingers, indicating that perhaps I'd held the piglet longer than I should have done. I reunited him with his mother and we followed Patrick into the house.

When I got back from the bathroom Annette was installed at the kitchen table and Patrick had got down a huge, frying pan and was melting some butter. He opened the fridge and produced a plate of thick bacon rashers.

Annette and I exchanged glances.

Patrick laid the rashers tenderly in the frying pan. "Esmeralda. One of my best sows, she was. Used to come to her name if you called her. Bit like a dog. Pigs are a lot more intelligent than people give them credit for, you know."

"I think I'll just have eggs," Annette said.

"Me too. I'm not that hungry. Actually coffee would be fine for me."

Patrick looked at us. "I'm kidding you. This isn't really Esmeralda." He turned the bacon over and gave us an ironic smile. "What do you take me for?"

"Do you reckon it was Esmeralda?" I asked Annette, when we were driving away from Home Farm.

"Hard to tell with Patrick." She grinned. "He's got a bit of a strange sense of humour."

I shuddered. "He's a bit strange altogether, if you ask me. I don't think I'm ever going to eat bacon again."

"Me neither. Still, at least we can tick another thing off your list. Damn we forget to ask him about the horse shoeing. Shall I go back?"

"No, I think I'd like to do something simple next."

"I could dye your hair pink if you like. We can pick up a kit on the way back."

Chapter Four

Three hours later we were sitting in my kitchen. Annette had refused to let me look in the mirror throughout the proceedings and now I could see why.

"That's not pink," I said. "It's more purple."

"Purply pink. It suits you, though. Don't you think?"

"No."

"Shall I wash it out then?"

Several washes later the colour had softened to a mulberry colour and I was beginning to panic.

"I can't understand it." Annette picked up the packet. "It definitely says temporary on here."

"How temporary?"

"I don't know. I didn't read the small print."

I couldn't read it either. Not without a magnifying glass. I glanced back at my reflection in the mirror.

"It'll probably look better in natural light," Annette said hopefully. We went into the bedroom and I stood by the window with my hand mirror. In natural light, the colour was closer to puce.

"What am I going to do?"

"Wear a scarf?"

"It could be weeks. Anyway, it's the middle of summer. It's too hot."

"I'll take you to my salon," Annette said. "Marcus will be able to sort you out. He's brilliant. I'll ring now and book an appointment." She came back from the phone, smiling. "He can fit us in in half an hour. Come on, I'll drive you."

"What if we see someone on the way?" I muttered as we went downstairs.

"We won't see anyone. You can duck down in the back of the car." She grabbed a yellow plastic raincoat from the stand in the hallway. "That's got a hood. Put that on just in case."

I buttoned the raincoat up and put up the hood, but it was only when we were halfway down the road that I realised I'd still got my slippers on.

"We'll have to go back. I can't go to the salon with no shoes."

Annette sighed and turned the car round and parked outside the house. "Tell me where they are and I'll go and get them."

I gave her the door key and watched her let herself in. This was ludicrous. Totally, utterly ludicrous. After I'd got my hair restored to its usual dark brown I was going to screw up the stupid list and chuck it in the bin. I couldn't believe I'd let Annette talk me into it in the first place. There were much better ways of proving I was my own person again. Much better ways of proving I was over Robert.

Movement in the rear view mirror caught my attention. A car was pulling up on the other side of the road. I looked at the familiar number plate and felt suddenly numb. Robert's car. He wasn't alone either. I could see Madeline, my ex mother in law, sitting in the passenger seat. What on earth were they doing here? Robert had no reason to come round. His post was forwarded and there wasn't an item of his stuff left in the house. I'd made sure of that. I shuddered. They'd have to walk right past me and Robert would recognise Annette's car. If I stayed here he was going to spot me. He couldn't really miss me. And I'd either have to keep my hood up or let him see my purple hair. I could just imagine the look on his face. Not to mention Madeline's. I could hear his condescending voice. *"Whatever are you doing, Wendy? See, I told you she'd go off the rails if we got divorced."*

Perhaps he was right. Perhaps I had gone off the rails. Making a split second decision, I flung open the car door and ran. My heart was thudding frantically as I tore up to the front door of the house. Annette had shut it behind her and I couldn't afford to hang around. Behind me a car door slammed and I could hear Madeline's voice clearly. "What if she's not in, Robert?"

At least they hadn't spotted me so far.

"Someone's in. I just saw the curtain move in the bedroom."

So Annette knew they were here too. What would she do? I abandoned all hope of her opening the front door in time for me to slip in unnoticed and ran to the side gate instead. Slamming it behind me, I raced round to the back door. Annette would come round and open that. Of course she would.

I heard the doorbell ring. Two sharp bursts. Robert had never had any patience. Then he clattered the letterbox. "Come on, Wendy, I know you're in. I only want a quick word."

Go away, I prayed. Why, oh why did they have to come round now?

The letterbox clattered again. "For pity's sake, Wendy, stop playing silly games and let us in." This was followed by another long ring on the doorbell.

What was Annette doing in there? Why didn't she let me in the back way? I tapped softly on the glass door.

At the same moment, I heard Robert say, "Oh, well if that's the way she wants to play it, I'll just have to help myself. I expect the side gate's open and she never locks the shed."

"I don't think we ought to…" Madeline's voice was doubtful. "Not without at least letting her know. We just want to pick up Robert's tools, love," she called through the letterbox. "We won't be two ticks. Is that all right?"

I glanced around me frantically. Now, what was I going to do? There was absolutely nowhere to hide in the garden. Not even a bush. How was I going to explain what I was doing on the patio with purple hair, wearing my slippers and a raincoat?

I didn't need to explain myself. I had every right to wear exactly what I liked in my own garden. I was confident. I was the kind of girl who could buy freezers and jump off the top diving board. *Fall off the top diving board*, said a mocking little voice in my head. Robert's voice. And then I heard it for real.

"Oh, come on, Mum. I haven't got time to stand here all day. Let's just help ourselves."

I couldn't face them. I just couldn't. The wheelie bin stood by the back door. It was empty and I'd disinfected it last bin day. I'd get in there. They'd never know. Perhaps I'd better take my raincoat off. It would be a bit hot with the lid down. But, then I heard footsteps and I knew there wasn't time.

I was installed seconds before the gate opened and I heard their voices, quieter now.

"Are you sure she won't mind, Robert? What if she calls the police? I mean, technically we are trespassing."

"She won't mind. And I'm not leaving those tools behind. She's stung me for enough money already."

Cheek, I thought, listening to their footsteps going towards the shed. I'd forgotten about Robert's gardening tools. He was living in a flat now and couldn't possibly need them. But he was right, the shed was open. It would only take a few minutes and then they'd go and I'd be safe. Annette was going to die of laughter when I told her what I'd had to do to avoid them.

Heck, it was baking in here. Dark too, and the smell of disinfectant was overpowering. There was still a bit of it left in the bottom, I could feel its dampness going through the soles of my slippers. I unbuttoned the raincoat and pulled the hood down. I'd pass out if I didn't get a bit of air soon.

"Right, that's all of them, I think." Robert's voice carried clearly across the garden. "Can you manage that box, Mum. It's not heavy. I'll bring the spade and the other bits and pieces."

There was a scraping sound as he put the tools down and then a thud, which I couldn't identify.

"Damn. This broom's seen better days. The handle needs gluing back in properly. Hmm, maybe not. Half the bristles have rotted through. I don't think I'll bother taking this."

"Well, don't just leave it there," Madeline said. "Pick it up."

"I don't want this ratty old thing in my car."

"I'm sure Wendy doesn't want it in her shed either."

There was a pause and I felt a trickle of sweat run down my back. I screwed my eyes up tight, my heart going into overdrive. No, please, no. Life couldn't be that cruel.

The Wish List

"Pick it up, Robert," Madeline urged. "There's a wheelie bin by the back door, we can pop it in there on our way out."

☑ Chapter Five

My heart pounded as their footsteps came closer. Maybe this was some kind of nightmare and in a minute I'd wake up. But it was far too vivid to be a nightmare. Not to mention far too hot. I racked my brain for a logical explanation as to why I might be crouched in my own wheelie bin, wearing my slippers and a raincoat in the middle of summer. I couldn't think of one. I closed my eyes and braced myself for the lid to open. For Robert's mother to peer in and say, *"Wendy, dear, what ARE you doing?"* Maybe the best plan would be to pretend I really had gone stark, staring mad. They weren't going to need a lot of convincing after finding me in here. I could manage a bit of hysterical laughter, no problem. I was close to it already.

And then, just before they reached the wheelie bin, I heard Annette's voice, loud and authoritative. "I suppose you're aware that you're trespassing and that I've just called the police."

"Well, we did ring the bell," Robert said. Even, caught wrong footed, as he was, he was an expert at turning situations round so that you were in the wrong and not him. He'd done it to me for years.

"That's right and no one answered." Madeline sounded aggrieved and it struck me where he'd got it from.

"Which most people would take as an indication that no one was in," Annette said in her most sarcastic voice. "Now, I think you'd better put that lot back before the police get here."

"But they're mine."

"Ah, but I've only got your word for that. And until Wendy gets back and can confirm whose they are, I suggest you do as I say."

I smiled. I should have realised that Annette would be more than a match for my ex-husband and the mother in law from hell.

"Where is Wendy anyway?" Robert sounded petulant.

"Out of the country," Annette said, without hesitation. "I'm house sitting until she gets back. I'll ask her to call you, shall I?"

For a minute I thought he was going to argue. It wasn't like him to back down to anyone. But Madeline knew when she was beaten.

"She's right, Robert," she snapped. "Now, come on."

I listened with relief to their retreating footsteps. I hoped they weren't going to take too long putting the tools back. I was beginning to feel sick.

A few seconds later, to my great relief, I heard the shed door slam, followed by the crash of the side gate. Robert was evidently not best pleased at having his plans thwarted. Thank you, God, I murmured. It was only just in time. I wasn't far from passing out. I stood up, intending to open the lid, and overbalanced. Or perhaps I skidded on what was left of the disinfectant. When I tried to right myself, the wheelie bin begin to tip and then the whole thing went over, hitting the ground with a crash. I think I might have yelped, but the next thing I was truly aware of was Annette's incredulous voice saying, "Wendy, this might be a silly question, but what are you doing in there?"

I couldn't answer her. I lay on my back, half in, half out of the bin, looking up into the summer blue sky, torn between tears and laughter.

She crouched beside me. "Are you OK?"

I gulped air. "Can you make sure they've gone?"

She scrambled to her feet and went to the gate. A few moments later she was back. "They've definitely gone."

"Thank heavens for that." I extricated myself from the bin, unpeeled the yellow raincoat and kicked off my slippers, which were soaked through with disinfectant. "Phew, that was close, Annette. You can't imagine how relieved I was to hear your voice. I thought they were going to find me."

She looked at me, still incredulous. "Then she bent and picked up the sodden slippers. "I'll chuck these, shall I?"

"Good idea. Have you really called the police?"

"No."

"Well, that's a blessing." I sat up, rubbing my back. "I think I've pulled a muscle."

"Was that getting into the bin, or falling out of it?"

"Goodness knows? Does it matter?"

"No, I don't suppose it does." She met my eyes and simultaneously we began to laugh. I wasn't sure whether it was delayed shock or sheer relief, but for a few moments neither of us could speak. We just collapsed in fits of laughter on my patio. Annette was the first to be able to string a coherent sentence together.

"I think we might have missed your hair appointment," she said.

A few days later the whole episode seemed a bit surreal. It was hard to believe it had even happened except that I still had purple hair. We had missed the appointment and I hadn't got round to booking another. It didn't seem as important any more. The colour faded a little more with each wash and I'd decided I could live with it. I'd also decided to chuck away the list.

"It's caused enough trouble already," I told Annette. We were sitting in her kitchen drinking cappuccinos.

"Ah," she said. "I was afraid you were going to say that." She paused and then went on sheepishly. "The thing is - I've arranged for you to go and shoe a horse at Patrick's."

"When?"

"Saturday morning. You don't have to go, of course." She sipped her coffee and studied me. "But it seems a shame not to - now I've arranged it." She flushed. She looked edgy, although I couldn't quite fathom out why.

The thought of seeing Pig Farmer Patrick again was not particularly appealing, but it did seem mean to refuse point blank, seeing as Annette had taken the trouble to organize it. I hadn't chucked away the list either. Annette had persuaded me to keep it for posterity.

☑ Chapter Six

At least it was sunny on Saturday. Home Farm looked brighter than I remembered. Most of the neglect was due to lack of funds, I observed, as we waited for Patrick to answer the bell. A coat of paint and new windows would make a big difference.

"Morning, ladies." Patrick was wearing the same blue boiler suit he'd had on last time, although it looked a little cleaner. He smiled and led us through the kitchen, which thankfully now smelt quite normal, and out into the courtyard where we'd seen Dora and her family.

Opposite the barn was a row of stables, all empty, with their bottom doors closed and their top doors hooked open. An enormous shaggy brown and white horse was tied up alongside one of them.

"This is Munster," Patrick said. "He's as quiet as they come, so if you're going to shoe a horse, then he's a good one to start with. The farrier will be along in about ten minutes. Fancy some breakfast while you're waiting?"

"No thanks," Annette and I said, simultaneously.

"Fair dos." Patrick grinned at us, raised one eyebrow and added, "Like the hair, Wendy, it suits you."

"Do you think he was serious?" I whispered to Annette, once he was out of earshot.

She frowned. "Who knows?"

The farrier arrived, introduced himself as John, and started lugging equipment out of his van. He was a tiny little man with white hair and wrinkles and looked about seventy, but maybe that was just a lifetime spent outdoors.

"I'm replacing the near hind," he told us. "Cast it yesterday."

Annette and I nodded knowledgeably, although I don't think she had any more clue as to what he was talking about than I had.

He didn't speak to us again, just began hammering away at his mobile anvil. Munster didn't seem remotely interested in what was going on. He dozed, his huge head drooping in the sunshine. It was hot again. I was feeling quite sleepy myself, when suddenly John shouted, "OK, Wendy. We're just about ready."

I went obediently to where he stood, just to one side of Munster's hindquarters.

"Done owt like this before?"

I shook my head.

"Can't let you bang the nails in. One wrong move and you'll cripple him for life. You can hold his leg up for me. I'll give you a quick demo." He tapped Munster's back leg and said, "Up." And the horse obligingly lifted it.

"Easy as that, see. All I need you to do is hold on tight."

"Right."

I copied what he'd done and Munster, rather to my surprise, let me pick up his hoof. It was the size of a dinner plate and I held it gingerly, one hand underneath, as I'd been shown.

John nodded his approval and began filing away with a great big metal file.

I hadn't realised that horses' legs were so heavy. Or maybe Munster was taking advantage of the fact that I was supporting his leg and had started to lean on me. Whatever it was, after about thirty seconds my arms had gone numb. I hung on determinedly until at last, John said, "That'll do for now," and I let go in relief.

Annette was sitting on a mounting block, watching with interest. "You look a bit hot, Wendy."

The Wish List

"Not at all." I grinned at her. "You were right. It's by far the easiest thing on my list."

It did occur to me, just after I'd spoken, that I probably shouldn't have said that. Bearing in mind what had happened with the rest of the list, it was perhaps just a teeny bit too much of a temptation for fate. But it did seem easy. Munster was relaxed. The sun was out. Everything was going according to plan.

John was just lining up the shoe to bang in the first nail when one of Patrick's collies shot across the yard after a cat. The cat, realising it was in a dead end, launched itself into the air and over the stable door that Munster was tied up next to. The horse couldn't have seen it until the last minute. And then it must have been a bit of a shock. An airborne ginger fur ball heading straight for your head.

The first indication I had of things going wrong was when the leg I was holding, jerked violently and the shoe that John was putting on, flew through the air and hit the stable door. I was propelled in the same direction, at roughly the same speed and I also hit the stable door, I think. It happened so quickly that all I was really aware of was John swearing loudly and then of finding myself horizontal on the concrete yard, looking up at Patrick, who was bending over me.

"Are you all right, Wendy?" Where had he come from? In the background I could hear Annette's anxious voice.

"I think she hit her head."

"I didn't."

"Better stay lying down just in case." Patrick pushed me gently, but firmly, back onto the ground, but he needn't have bothered. My surroundings were spinning in on me. And I don't remember a lot after that. So, perhaps they were right. Perhaps I had hit my head.

Some time later I woke up on my back. I was on a narrow bed with screens around me. A hospital, I thought, but as consciousness returned, so did confusion. A stream of images fast forwarded through my head. Losing my bikini top in a swimming pool, crouching in a dustbin in a raincoat, and something about having pink hair. Somewhere, amongst the images, there was a thread of coherent thought. Hadn't I at some point decided I was losing my marbles? Maybe that was what had happened. Maybe I was now lying in a psychiatric hospital.

My head certainly felt fuzzy enough. I closed my eyes again.

The next time I risked opening them, everything looked much the same, except this time I heard Annette's voice.

"Oh, you're back in the land of the living, are you? How are you feeling?"

"Fine." I sat up, and instantly regretted it. Hangover was not the word for it. Odd, I couldn't remember drinking anything, but I'd very clearly been drinking far too much of something. "Was it a good party?" I said to Annette.

"Party?" She looked alarmed.

"You mean we haven't been to a party?"

"No." She leaned towards me and her face blurred. "Tell me exactly what you remember."

"Only if you promise not to tell anyone," I said, and giggled.

Annette's look of alarm deepened. "Wendy, stop messing about and tell me."

"Only if you promise." I wagged a finger at her and lowered my voice. "I don't want to stay in here for the rest of my life. Once they get you in these places they never let you out again you know."

She shuffled her chair a bit closer to the bed. She didn't look alarmed any more, just a bit puzzled, but all she said was, "All right, I promise."

I told her in hushed tones exactly what I remembered, starting with the missing bikini top and ending with the dustbin.

"You don't remember anything about shoeing a horse?" Annette asked when I'd finished.

I frowned at her, wondering briefly if she was part of some massive hallucination. "No. Can I ask you something now?"

"Of course."

"And you'll give me a straight answer?"

"Yes."

"Have I got pink hair?"

She nodded. "Well, it's more purple than pink." But before she could say anything else a nurse came into the room.

"How is she?"

"She's absolutely fine," Annette said. "Except she can't remember the accident."

"Well, that's normal after a bump on the head. I expect it will come back to her sooner or later."

"So you're not going to keep me in here for weeks on end?" I interrupted, and the nurse smiled.

"Absolutely not. We need the bed. Once the doctor has okayed it, you can go. Have you got someone at home to keep an eye on you?"

I nodded and Annette said, "No, she hasn't. But she can come and stay with me. I'll look after her."

"Where are we?" I hissed, as soon as the nurse went out of the room.

"Accident and emergency. We thought it best to get them to check you over."

"Have I been in an accident?"

Annette smiled reassuringly. "It's nothing to worry about. I'll fill you in later."

☑ Chapter Seven

Fortunately, she didn't need to. To my huge relief, my memory filtered back over the rest of the day, although I decided to stay at Annette's for a while anyway. The following evening we sat in her kitchen and she agreed with me that it was far too risky to attempt anything else on the list.

"I'm sorry I talked you into the horse shoeing," she said. "It's probably my fault that you ended up in hospital. You were all set to call it quits then, weren't you?"

I glanced at the piece of paper. "I've done most of these, anyway. Saving someone's life isn't something I can plan. The belly dancing's out because the course doesn't start in time and the other one I haven't done involves flying a plane." I raised my eyebrows. "I think we can safely say that one's out too."

"You could do number ten." Annette grinned. "I'd say Robert would be the perfect candidate for that."

"He thinks I'm out of the country," I reminded her. "Which suits me perfectly. I think I might stay abroad for quite a while."

As we were talking the doorbell rang.

"Are you expecting anyone?"

"No." She jumped up. She was gone ages and I was just about to get off the settee and go and see if she needed rescuing when the lounge door opened and Annette came back in, followed by Patrick.

"I said you were fine," she said, a note of impatience in her voice, "But he wouldn't take my word for it. He wanted to come and see for himself."

Patrick was dressed in jeans and a smart jacket and holding a small bunch of flowers. Out of his boiler suit and freshly shaved, he looked quite different and for the first time I could see why Annette had said he was tasty.

"Hi, Wendy. I wanted to drop by and apologise for what happened with Munster."

"It was hardly your fault."

"It was on my property. I feel responsible. I was wondering if I could take you out for a meal to make up for it." He turned to include Annette. "Both of you, I mean."

I was struggling for the words to say no, diplomatically, when Annette said, "Sounds lovely, Patrick. When did you have in mind?"

After the arrangements had been made and he'd gone I turned on her. "Why did you do that? I don't want to go out for a meal with him."

"Well, you don't have to come. You can drop out at the last minute if you like. But I happen to think he's rather fanciable."

"Annette, that's not on. Why involve me? I think you ought to phone him up right now and tell him it's just going to be you."

"He won't be home, yet," she said, but she had the grace to blush. Then she came across the room, "I'm sorry, Wendy, but I couldn't resist it. He might not want to come if he thinks it's just me."

There was something that sounded suspiciously like insecurity in her voice and I stared at her. I'd never heard Annette sounding insecure about anything, work, men, the way she looked. Nothing ever fazed her.

"I really like him," she said, sitting on the settee and not looking at me. "I know you think I'm ultra-confident, but it's not always how I feel – inside, I mean."

"It's not."

"No. Well, not lately anyway." She rested her chin on her hands and now she did look at me. "To be honest, Wendy, all I've felt lately is rather lonely."

After this revelation we spent the rest of the evening talking. I couldn't believe that I'd been so wrapped up in my own problems that I hadn't realised how she felt.

"You've always seemed so strong. I'm so sorry, Annette. I've been utterly selfish."

"You and me, both." She smiled ruefully. "Arranging for you to cuddle the piglet and the horse shoeing. Well, my motives weren't entirely altruistic. I was going to arrange for you to fly a remote control plane too. I was going to talk Patrick into letting me use one of his fields."

"But wouldn't it have been simpler just to ask him out?"

"I couldn't. What if he'd said no?"

"Why should he say no? Haven't you looked in the mirror lately? You're beautiful, Annette."

She smiled. "Thanks, but he's had plenty of opportunities to ask me out. He's in often enough. I thought he was shy, but now I'm not so sure. I think I might be too pushy for him. In fact, to be honest I think the whole thing's backfired on me. I think Patrick fancies *you*."

I nearly choked on my coffee. "You think he's into women with purple hair, do you?"

"He said it suited you." She sniffed and I was stunned to see a tear roll down her face.

"Annette, listen to me." I took her hand. "I'm sure he's very nice, but he's not my type."

"So you don't mind dropping out at the last minute?"

"I'd be delighted," I said.

Our date with Patrick was for the following Saturday, a week before my fortieth birthday. He'd offered to pick us both up, which I thought was rather sweet of him. Annette first and then me, although the plan was that I'd phone him on his mobile just before 7.00 to say I thought I was going down with something, leaving the coast clear for Annette.

"If you tell him any sooner he might change his mind and try and rearrange for another night," Annette had said. "So, it has to be last minute."

"Fine," I said.

Frankly I'd be glad when it was all over. By five o'clock on Saturday, Annette had been on the phone a dozen times.

"I think my black dress is too posh. I'm going for my brown trousers and silk shirt. No, I've changed my mind. I think Patrick's a 'leg man', so I'm going for my short skirt. Actually, no, it looks awfully short. He might think I'm a tart. Oh, I wish you were here, Wendy, I can't decide. I feel quite ill."

I made soothing noises, which seemed to work until the next phone call. "How about that red dress I bought at Melanie's?"

"Fine."

At quarter to seven she was back on the phone again. "Wendy, you're never going to believe this, but I've just thrown up."

"It's just nerves," I said. "Take some deep breaths."

She gave a low moan. "Oh no, I don't think it is," and the dial tone hummed in my ear.

Alarmed, I waited five minutes and called her back. I was on the point of giving up when she answered it. "Are you all right, Annette?"

"No. I think I'm coming down with something. I'm going to have to phone Patrick. I can't let him see me looking like this. It'll put him off for life."

"We'll arrange it for another time," I told her. "Don't worry."

I'd just put the phone down when the doorbell rang. When I went to answer it I found Patrick clutching another bunch of flowers. My surprise must have been written all over my face, or maybe it was the fact that I was wearing an ancient pair of leggings and a pink tee shirt with the words *Hug Me* emblazoned across the chest, that contributed to his puzzled expression. Not exactly 'going out' clothes, but then I hadn't been planning to go out.

"Am I too early?" he said.

"I thought you were picking up Annette first."

"You were the closest." As he followed me into my lounge his mobile rang.

I pretended not to listen as he made sympathetic noises. What the hell was I going to do now? If I said I'd gone down with the same thing as Annette, he was going to think this was some sort of wind up.

He disconnected and said, "Annette's not feeling too well. So it looks as though it's just going to be you and me."

"Oh dear, perhaps we should make it another evening?"

He considered this. "I suppose we could, but the table's booked. It would be a shame to waste it." He took a step towards me. He looked nice tonight too. I couldn't think why I'd ever thought he looked like the farmer on the Vicar of Dibley.

"I'm sorry Annette's not well," he began, "but actually I'm pleased it's just the two of us."

"You are?"

"Yes." He hesitated. "I knew the first time I saw you."

I stared at him in alarm. "Knew what?"

"That I wanted to get to know you better. You're gorgeous, Wendy. Hasn't anyone ever told you?" He clasped his hands together and took another step towards me.

"No. No, you mustn't say things like that. You can't. We can't." I backed away from him and tripped over the glass coffee table. And the next thing I knew I was lying on the floor in my lounge, looking up at him with this surreal feeling of déjà vu.

"Are you all right?" He was on his knees beside me. "You really must stop throwing yourself at my feet like this."

For a moment I thought he was being serious and then I saw the glint of humour in his eyes.

"Did you hurt yourself?"

I shook my head and sat up, which was a mistake, because his face was only inches from mine and suddenly I knew he was going to kiss me. At the last second I turned my head and his lips landed on my ear. And at precisely the same moment both my telephone and my doorbell rang.

☑ Chapter Eight

"Ignore them," Patrick said.

"I can't." I scrambled away from him, crawled on all fours across the carpet and got up, feeling as shaky as a jelly. Although whether that was down to the after effects of falling over again or the shock of what Patrick had just said, I wasn't sure.

The answer machine cut in to get the phone, but the doorbell rang again. I charged along the hallway, praying that it would be Annette, fully recovered, and swung back the front door.

Robert stood there, arms behind his back. "Ah, Wendy, you're back. Or maybe you never went. Thought that feminist friend of yours was probably spinning me a story. Good God, whatever have you done with your hair?" A nasty smile played over his face. "Oh, I get it. You were too ashamed to go out looking like that, so you've been hiding."

Attack had always been Robert's first line of defence, but, even though I knew this, I could feel myself crumbling under his condescending gaze. Before I could say anything, however, I heard the lounge door open and Patrick came up behind me, put his arms around my waist and said, "Is this moron bothering you, Wendy?"

Robert's sneer evaporated so quickly that it was hard not to laugh. Patrick was about six inches taller than him and had strong muscular forearms. I hadn't noticed them before, but they were currently wrapped around my waist and were hard to miss.

Acting on instinct and without stopping to consider the consequences, I turned my head and said, "Yes, darling, I think he's trying to sell something, but I've told him I'm not interested."

"Maybe he needs telling a bit louder," Patrick said, letting go of me and advancing towards the open door.

Robert didn't hang around to argue. I'd never seen him move so fast. He was out on the street and unlocking his car before Patrick had time to get down the step. The car screeched off up the road and Patrick came back in with a smile on his face.

"Thank you."

"My pleasure." He raised his eyebrows and added wickedly, "Darling."

I blushed. "That was just for Robert's benefit. I didn't mean anything by it. Look, Patrick, the thing is, I don't... I mean I can't."

"It's all right." He put a hand on my arm. "You don't need to spell it out. I think I've got the picture. I'll just get my jacket and I'll be out of your hair."

I followed him back into the lounge. "At least let me make you a coffee. I truly am grateful for what you did just now. Robert's my ex-husband."

"I guessed he was. Annette told me you'd just got divorced. By the way that was her on the answer machine." He picked up his jacket and smiled at me.

"So, will you stay for coffee?"

"If you're sure I won't be outstaying my welcome?"

"I'm sure," I said, realising with surprise that I was. I'd pigeonholed Patrick from the moment I'd seen him. I'd had him down as a rather unaware, slow witted clod. I'd mistaken his ironic sense of humour for insensitivity. But there was nothing slow about the way he'd just interpreted the situation with Robert, or the way he'd acted. I felt a bit ashamed of myself.

He was watching me and I had the unnerving feeling that he knew exactly what I was thinking. To cover my confusion I turned away from him and busied myself filling up the kettle and spooning coffee into mugs.

Then I carried them back into the lounge and put them on the coffee table. I sat on the settee and Patrick sat in the armchair and for a while neither of us spoke. It wasn't an uncomfortable silence, though, and I found myself wondering if I'd have felt differently about him if I hadn't known that Annette was so enamoured.

"So have you ever been married?"

"How long have you known Annette?"

We spoke at the same moment and Patrick indicated that I should go first. I repeated the question and he told me that he'd married young, but that his wife hadn't liked farming life, which had turned out to be far more hard work than her idealistic fantasy of it. She'd upped and left after two years and he'd had to get a loan in order to give her her share of the house.

I couldn't see Annette as a farmer's wife either, I thought ruefully. She didn't like getting her hands dirty, although her money would certainly have transformed Patrick's farm.

"How about you?" Patrick asked. "How long were you married to Robert?"

I told him and he was such a good listener that I somehow ended up telling him about the list as well.

"That explains a lot," he murmured, although I wasn't sure if he meant he now understood why we'd kept turning up at his farm with strange requests, or that he understood why I'd felt the need to work my way through the list in the first place.

"The plan was that I do as many things as possible before my fortieth birthday."

"Which is when?"

"Next Saturday." I got the list out and showed him. "I was going to chuck it away. It's turned into a bit of a fiasco, but Annette said I ought to keep it for posterity.

It was the last time either of us mentioned Annette. We drunk more coffee and we relaxed in each other's company and suddenly I realised that we'd been talking for more than three hours.

"I really have outstayed my welcome now," Patrick said, and I went with him to the front door, feeling curiously reluctant to say goodbye.

"If you have any more trouble with unwelcome salesmen, give me a call."

"Thanks, I will." We both smiled and I realised, with a little shock, that if he tried to kiss me again, I'd have let him.

But he didn't. He just said, "By the way, I really do like your hair that colour."

Feeling deflated I went back into the lounge and spotted the red light flashing on the machine. It was a bit late to phone Annette, especially if she still felt ill, but at least I could play back her message.

"Wendy, pick up the phone. Come on, I know you're there." There was a pause while she waited for me to comply. Then an exaggerated sigh. "I'll kill you if you've gone out with Patrick on your own. I saw him first and I'm madly in lust, so hands off. Phone me as soon as you get back."

I closed my eyes. Annette was going to be mortified when she found out that Patrick had heard all this. At least she hadn't said anything too incriminating. I was about to switch off the tape when she started speaking again. "I know you said he reminded you of that weirdo farmer on the Vicar of Dibley." She giggled and I felt my cheeks flame. "But you've got to admit he scrubs up well. Don't you think he's even a little bit tasty? Or has that moron ex-husband

embittered you forever? Call me later. Byeee."
The tape rewound and I closed my eyes.

Patrick's words as he came out of my lounge, echoed in my ears, *"Is this moron bothering you, Wendy?"* So I couldn't even kid myself that he hadn't heard what Annette had said. No wonder he'd backed off, having had my opinion of him chucked in his face with such casual brutality. He'd still come to my rescue though, hadn't he? In fact, unlike Annette and I, Patrick had been rather magnanimous tonight.

I went to bed, but I couldn't sleep. The image of Patrick bending over me as I lay on the carpet replayed itself over and over. I'd panicked because Annette liked him and because I wasn't used to being told I was gorgeous. Robert had spent so long finding fault that I'd begun to believe I couldn't do anything.

In the end I got up and went downstairs. The list was on the coffee table. I sat on the settee and read it through again. I'd even mucked this up. Far from finding my confidence I felt worse than ever. And then I cried for all the wasted time; for all that might have been if I'd had the courage to leave Robert earlier. I cried until there were no more tears left and then I tore the list into tiny pieces and fell asleep where I was on the settee.

☑ Chapter Nine

"Well, perhaps it turned out for the best," Annette said. It was Friday lunchtime, a week later and the day before my birthday. We were sitting outside a café, drinking our third mango smoothie. "You're right, I'd never had made a farmer's wife. In fact, I don't think I'm wife material at all. I'd have liked to go out with him a couple of times, though."

"You still could."

"No, I don't think so. Not now he knows how I feel about him. It would be too embarrassing."

"I'd have thought that would simplify things. No games, no pretence."

She smiled. "Nah. It was a nice fantasy, but I think I'm too much of a commitment phobic for Patrick. He's not going to go for a goodtime girl like me."

I didn't say anything. I hadn't told her what Patrick had said to me. There didn't seem much point, as I wasn't likely to see him again. I still felt a bit guilty that I'd enjoyed his company so much.

"Anyway..." She gave me a wide smile. "What time am I picking you up tomorrow and what are you wearing?"

"Half sevenish, if that's OK and I don't know. I don't feel much like celebrating."

"Look on it as a fresh start. Who knows, we might meet the men of our dreams while we're out."

We were going to a new Thai restaurant that Annette had discovered. If it hadn't been for her I'd have gone to bed early with a bar of chocolate and a good book.

When we got there I rather wished I had. The place was packed and it took ages to get served. The waiter had just taken our order and disappeared when there was a commotion on the table beside us. I glanced across and saw a woman in a patterned dress and pearls sitting opposite her bald headed husband. It was the man who had the problem. He was doubled over, making jerky movements, his face almost on his plate. His wife stood up, fluttering her hands to attract someone's attention, but there were no waiters in sight and the rest of the room seemed oblivious.

"Crikey, is he having a heart attack?" Annette said

"No, he's not." There was something about the man's movements that triggered a memory from my long ago First Aid training.

"He's choking." I stood up. No one else seemed to know what to do and the man was starting to turn an odd colour. I tapped his wife on the shoulder. "Did something go down the wrong way?"

"I don't know. He was fine. We were talking." She spoke in little gasps, her face uncomprehending.

They were eating steak, I saw. I hadn't done a First Aid course for years, but I could still remember that steak was the biggest cause of choking. I could also remember exactly what to do. I thumped the man between the shoulder blades. Three times. Nothing. I grabbed him from behind and clasped my hands below his ribcage and hoped I'd get the manoeuvre right. It didn't work the first time, but on the second attempt, something shot out of his mouth and hit the edge of the table.

The restaurant had gone quiet, I realised, with embarrassment. The room around us gradually tuning in to the little drama and a waiter, finally alerted, was hurrying across.

"Is everything all right, sir? Madam?"

I could feel my face flaming as I slipped back to our table where Annette was sitting open mouthed. "Where did you learn that?"

"First Aid course."

"Blimey." She leaned across and said in a hushed voice, "I think you probably just saved his life. And you're only just forty."

I smiled. "I was trying to forget about that."

"The list or being forty?"

"Both."

"He might turn out to be a millionaire who wants to reward you handsomely," Annette said.

"I doubt it."

And then our main courses arrived and the next time I looked, the couple had gone.

"They could at least have said thank you," Annette said huffily. "Or sent over a bottle."

"They were probably too embarrassed and wanted to go home," I murmured. "So make sure you chew your steak properly, I don't want a repeat performance."

Annette giggled. "I'd never have the nerve to do what you just did."

"It was instinct, not nerve."

Ignoring this, she said slyly, "After that I should think number ten would be a breeze. I mean, if you *were* going to do anything else on the list."

"Well, I'm not. Annette, if I'd had the nerve to do number ten I'd have left Robert years ago."

"He'd have left you, you mean. If it's any consolation, I couldn't do it either. I think it's probably the hardest one. Are we having dessert?"

She finally dropped me home just after midnight, declining my offer of coffee, which was a relief. All I wanted to do was crawl into bed and sleep. I let myself in and stepped over an envelope on the mat. Hand delivered. A late birthday card by the look of it. For one horrible moment I thought it might have been from Robert, but it turned out to be from Patrick. A surge of pleasure went through me, dampened by regret that I'd been out when he called. I'd phone him tomorrow and say thank you.

But the next day I remembered that I didn't know his number and I could hardly ask Annette for it. I knew where he lived, but calling round to say thank you for a birthday card seemed a bit over the top. He might get the wrong idea. But was it the wrong idea murmured a treacherous little voice in my mind? I'd hardly got him out of my thoughts all week. Perhaps I should just admit what I'd been trying to deny ever since he'd kissed my ear in the lounge. I very much wanted to see Patrick again.

And then an even more maddening thought crept into my head. I could kill two birds with one stone if I went to see him. I could tick off number ten. Not that I was attempting to complete the list, of course, but….

I decided to go that morning before I could change my mind.

☑ Chapter Ten

It was raining when I parked outside Home Farm. A fine grey mist that was doing its best to deny summer. I rang the doorbell, feeling sure there was no need. My heart was hammering loudly enough for Patrick to hear it, even if he was outside.

"Hello, Wendy." He was wearing his boiler suit again, but somehow all I could see now was the deep brown of his eyes and the way his mouth turned up slightly at one corner, giving him a perpetually ironic smile.

"I came to say thank you for my birthday card."

"There was no need." He didn't look surprised to see me, but neither did he show any signs of inviting me in. I could see this was going to be trickier than I'd thought.

"I don't suppose I could have a quick word?"

"You can join me for breakfast if you like." He turned and I followed him into the kitchen, which looked rather cleaner than it had the last time I'd seen it.

"Coffee?"

"Please." Now I was here, I didn't have a clue how to begin. It had seemed so obvious earlier. Number Ten was clear in my mind. *Tell a man exactly what you think of him. No holds barred.*

Patrick handed me a mug of coffee. "So what can I do for you, Wendy? Was it something else on your list you needed help with?"

Startled, I looked at him and then realised that he wasn't reading my mind. He'd seen the list too.

"I don't think I've got any planes lying about the place that you could fly," he went on, "But you'd be welcome to spend a night in one of my fields if you wanted to."

I smiled. "I'm not in a hurry to do either of those, but thanks for the offer."

He sipped his coffee. His face was deadpan and I decided that I might just as well plunge in.

"Actually, I wanted to apologise for what I said about you to Annette. You shouldn't have had to hear that on the answer phone."

"Ah."

"And I don't know why I ever said it, because it isn't what I think about you at all. Well not now anyway. You don't look anything like well er…" I tailed off, knowing that my face was burning, but he just looked amused.

"I haven't lost any sleep over it," he said. "So I shouldn't worry about it too much. More coffee?"

"No, I think I'd better go."

He came with me to the door. I don't know what I'd been expecting. That he'd ask to see me again, that he'd say he still liked me. Men's egos were fragile things. Living with Robert had taught me that. And I'd already trampled well and truly on Patrick's. He might appear to be indifferent, but he was probably finding this visit as excruciating as I was.

At the door I hesitated. No holds barred meant I should also tell him I really liked him and wanted to see him again. But I couldn't bring myself to say either of these things. I just stood there feeling like a fool.

"Thanks for coming round, Wendy."

"No problem." And I fled back to my car.

Half an hour later I was sitting in Annette's kitchen pouring out my heart to her.

"I didn't mean it to happen. I'm really sorry."

"But nothing has happened," Annette looked puzzled. "Unless there's something you're not telling me."

I shook my head.

"So, let's get this straight. Patrick said he liked you, you fell over the coffee table and then you told each other your life stories. Basically that was it?"

"Er, yes."

"Well, I can't see what you're worried about." She touched my hand. "I know you're not going to agree with me, but you've come a lot further these past three weeks than you think. You've conquered your fear of heights, you've saved someone's life and you've changed your image." She smiled. "And Patrick's right, that colour does suit you. Not to mention the fact that you've sent Robert packing and told a man you hardly know that you like him."

"But that's the point, I didn't."

"You don't need to spell these things out. I should think Patrick got the message when you turned up on his doorstep. I expect he's leaving a message on your answer machine as we speak."

"Do you think so?"

"Yes, but even if he isn't, it doesn't matter." She gave me a stern look. "The important thing is that you've moved on, which was the whole point, wasn't it? OK, maybe some of the stuff on your list didn't work out quite as planned, but you had the guts to do it. I wouldn't have done it." Her face softened. "Look what a wimp I was when I thought I fancied Patrick." Her clear green eyes held mine.

"I wouldn't have done it either, without you egging me on."

"Yeah, you would. You'd have done it all sooner or later."

☑ Chapter Eleven

I went home feeling a great deal better. The catharsis of confession maybe, because I'd felt guilty all week about liking Patrick. However vehemently Annette assured me that it had just been a crush, I didn't believe that she'd changed her mind so utterly.

I walked into my lounge and even though I'd been half expecting it, it was a shock to see the message light flashing on the answer machine.

It was a bigger shock to play the tape and find that the message wasn't from Patrick, but Robert.

"If it's OK with you, I'd like to come and pick up my tools some time. Give me a ring. Please."

I smiled. Robert saying please – that was a first. I phoned him before I could chicken out and told him I'd leave everything he wanted in the front garden and that as it was raining, he'd better get round pretty sharpish. A surge of adrenaline fuelled confidence flooded through me as I put the phone down. I'd never have dared to speak to him like that before. Annette was right, I wasn't the same person I'd been

The Wish List

three weeks ago. Somewhere along the way, something had changed. It was a revelation.

Ten minutes later I'd put the last of Robert's possessions, including the rotten broom handle that had so nearly been my undoing, into a big black bin liner and left it by the front gate. The phone was ringing as I went back into the house, but the answer machine cut in before I could pick it up.

"Hello, Wendy, it's Patrick here. Further to what we were talking about this morning, I thought I'd mention that if you still wanted to go skinny-dipping then you'd be very welcome to use my duck pond. It's a bit weedy and there's not a lot of water in at the moment, but it's getting fuller by the minute." He paused and I went across to pick up the phone.

"That's a disgraceful suggestion to make," I said, keeping my voice as deadpan as his. "I've a good mind to report you for making obscene phone calls."

"Wendy. I – er – didn't mean." It was the first time I'd ever heard him sound unsure of himself. "I'm sorry. I was joking."

"I see. Well in that case I think it would be more appropriate for you to apologise in person.

So I can satisfy myself that you're being sincere."

He coughed. "Of course. I'll er come over. I've got to see a man about a pig over your way."

How romantic, I thought. Or perhaps he was joking about that too. As Annette had said, when she'd first introduced us, it was hard to tell.

Fifteen minutes later he arrived on my doorstep. "I'd like to offer my sincere apologies," he began gravely.

"Accepted," I said, equally gravely. He turned to go and I caught hold of his hand. "There was one more thing on my list that I needed your help with, as it happens."

"But not skinny dipping?" There was a definite glint in his dark eyes now.

"No." I took a deep breath. "I wanted to tell you that I'd like to see you again because actually I can't think of anything else I'd rather do. Unlike you, I didn't realise it the first time I saw you, but I was probably being a bit slow on the uptake."

"You're not slow on the uptake, Wendy," he said, a slow smile spreading across his face. "I'd say your timing is utterly perfect."

The Wish List

He stepped towards me at more or less the same moment that Robert drew up outside the house. As Robert bent to pick up the black bin liner of tools, Patrick bent to kiss me. I closed my eyes and gave myself up to the warmth of his lips and thought that maybe he was right. Maybe just for once, my timing was perfect, after all.

Della Galton

If You've Enjoyed This Book…

I hope you've enjoyed this book as much as I enjoyed writing it. This is just one of several novellas now available on amazon. Why not give '*Ten Weeks To Target*' a try? You can read Chapter One in a couple of pages time.

In the meantime, if you'd like to stay in touch or help me 'spread the word', then here are a few ways you can do just that:

'Like' my Facebook Page
Pop along to www.facebook.com/dailydella, and click the LIKE button (up there at the top). Your 'friends' will be able to see that you're a fan, and you might see a daily post from myself in your feed. Nothing too intrusive, I promise.

Follow me on Twitter
If you're more of a tweeter I tweet under the handle @dellagalton. The odd re-tweet would be most appreciated.
You can follow me here: twitter.com/dellagalton

The Wish List

Review this book
Positive reviews are always welcome. You don't have to have bought this book on amazon to leave a review.

Got a blog or a podcast?
A book review, or a link to my website (www.dellagalton.co.uk) are always appreciated. And if you'd like to interview me for your blog or podcast, just drop me a line.

Tell a friend
And finally, one of the hardest things for any author to achieve is 'word of mouth' recommendations. Next time you find yourself discussing books with a friend, please remember me! :-)

Lots of love
Della

Della Galton

Ten Weeks To Target

**ONE OF SEVERAL NOVELLAS BY DELLA GALTON.
NOW AVAILABLE AS AN EBOOK, AND IN PAPERBACK,
FROM AMAZON AND ALL GOOD BOOKSELLERS**

The Wish List

Ten Weeks To Target – Chapter One

"Why don't you just get a bigger size, Mum?"

Very good question, Janine thought as she struggled to get the zip done up on her jeans. Everything was so simple when you were fourteen, going on twenty-five, and could eat whatever you wanted without putting on a pound. She glanced at Kelly, who was sitting on the bed, her dark hair gelled into hedgehog spikes and her blue eyes impatient.

"Because I don't want a bigger size," she said patiently. "I want to fit into this size." Especially as your Aunt Alison will be looking like she's just stepped off a catwalk, she could have added, but didn't in case she sounded like a cow.

Alison was her sister in law. Alison was perfect. Well, she was in the looks department anyway. She had the sort of cheekbones photographers raved about, not a trace of a laughter line despite being in her mid forties – blond hair that always looked effortlessly styled and – most enviably of all in Janine's book right now – she was a size ten.

"If you're getting all done up for Aunt Ali's benefit then I shouldn't bother," Kelly went on with irritating perception. "She's far more interested in discussing the 'wedding of the year' than in what you look like."

"Yes, but that isn't the point," Janine said, forcing the button into place. It would be all right if she didn't sit down. And if she wore a long top then maybe she could leave the button undone. With a bit of luck Ali would be in too much of a rush to stop long.

"What do you think?" she said, spinning round in front of her daughter. "Do I look fat?"

"No-oo," Kelly said, spinning out the O in the way she did when she was trying to think of something diplomatic to say. "But you do look – er – uncomfortable."

Uncomfortable was the understatement of the year, Janine thought wryly, and she hadn't dared breathe out yet. Maybe it would be more sensible to wear her black trousers. At least they fitted properly. The trouble was, her sister in law was going to think she didn't have any other trousers.

And then the doorbell rang and it was suddenly too late. She checked her hair in the mirror. She always seemed to be too busy ferrying Kelly around to have time to worry about such things as hair appointments. Her shoulder length brown frizz was in dire need of a cut and grey was coming through at the sides. She was sure it hadn't been there yesterday. Why did it always have to come through just at the wrong time?

"Shall I let her in?" Kelly asked, standing up in one careless, graceful movement.

"Yes. No, I'll do it." Janine reached for her scent, at least she'd smell nice, but as she stretched forward, her jeans finally gave up the battle and tore along the crotch.

The bell rang again and Kelly hesitated in the bedroom doorway. "Oops, have they ripped?" she said sympathetically. "Why don't you wear your nice black ones instead."

Sometimes, Janine thought, swallowing the urge to scream, she could have sworn that Kelly was the pacifying adult and she the child.

"I'll let Aunt Ali in," Kelly added and disappeared.

Janine ripped off the ruined jeans and rifled frantically through her wardrobe. No black trousers. Suddenly remembering they were in the wash, she tore into the bathroom and found them screwed up in the bottom of the linen basket.

They'd pass if she ironed them, but the iron was downstairs and by now that's where Alison would be too – sitting slim and elegant in her kitchen. She must have something else that fitted. A frantic further search of her wardrobe told her different. It would have to be her tracksuit bottoms. She hauled them off the hanger, remembering belatedly that the last time she'd worn them had been to emulsion the spare room, which wasn't quite finished. They were paint spattered, but at least they fitted. She raced across the landing and put her head around the spare room door. A tray of paint brushes was laid out neatly on some newspaper. She grabbed one and went downstairs slowly.

Alison and Kelly were sitting at the kitchen table, bent over a wedding magazine. Janine put on her brightest smile.

"Hi, Ali, sorry I forgot you were coming, I was just – er – doing a bit of decorating." With a bit of luck she could pass off the grey in her hair as paint.

"Oh, don't let me stop you." Alison glanced up. She looked breath taking as usual in a navy and white suit. Positively nautical, Janine thought, which was perhaps why she felt a bit sick. Or perhaps that was because she was afraid that Kelly would give the game away and she'd have to confess that she had simply outgrown her wardrobe. All of it, without even noticing.

But all her darling daughter did was to raise her eyebrows and shake her head slightly. "I'll put the kettle on while you two talk weddings," she said, sliding off her chair and coming across the kitchen. She took the dry paintbrush out of Janine's hand. "And I'll put this in some white spirit, shall I, Mum, save it going all stiff and hard."

Fortunately Alison didn't seem too interested in the decorating. "I thought you'd like to see the place cards we finally decided on," she murmured, barely glancing at Janine. "What do you think? Gorgeous, aren't they?"

"Lovely," Janine agreed dutifully, looking at the pink and blue edged cards.

"They'll go in little gold place holders," Alison went on. "Mia thought you might like to see the seating layout, too. I think we've finally thrashed it out. You're going to be here." She pointed a pale pink fingernail. "Next to Mia's uncle Martin, remember him – he's just split up with his wife, too. Poor man was devastated."

Great, Janine thought. A table of discarded aunts and uncles, neatly packaged away by the fire exit by the look of it.

"It'll cheer him up sitting with you," Alison went on brightly. "Have you decided what you're going to wear yet?"

"Er no, I haven't had much time to think about it. What with the decorating."

"Well, chop chop, it's only ten weeks away now, you know. I've had my outfit for a year."

Janine nodded miserably and resisted the urge to confess that if she'd had her outfit for a year, she'd have had to let it out by at least three sizes by now. Some women gave up eating when they were unhappy, but unfortunately she'd never been one of them. Since she and Jonathan had separated she'd piled on weight like there was no tomorrow. Well, chocolate was so much more comforting than salad, wasn't it. But she felt quite unable to say any of this to Alison, who actually looked as if she'd lost weight lately.

"Mind you, I'll have to get it taken in," Alison muttered, flapping the waistband of her skirt. "What with all this running about I'm losing weight by the bucket load."

"What a nuisance," Janine said, hoping she didn't sound too bitter and twisted and reaching absently for the plate of chocolate hobnobs that Kelly had put out. "Have one of these?"

"Ugh, no thanks. Far too much on my mind to eat. Anyway, Janine dear, I'll leave you to your decorating. You're obviously up to your eyes in it. And, don't take this the wrong way, will you, but …" She hesitated. "I thought you might like to get your hair done before the wedding at my salon. Ritchie's an absolute marvel. My treat of course."

"That's very sweet of you," Janine said through gritted teeth.

"I'll see myself out," Alison trilled, gathering up her place settings and slipping them into her slimline, designer handbag.

Janine was very tempted to slam the door behind her. Hard, so that it rattled the foundations of the house. Hard enough to get rid of some of the simmering frustration that threatened to burst out of her as tears.

"She means well," Kelly said, reading her mother's face as they came back into the kitchen. "And you'll look great whatever you wear."

"Thank you, darling." She treated her daughter to a hug, breathing in the mix of hair gel and apple shampoo and feeling a mixture of despair that she was a fat and frumpy forty year old, and relief that she had such a gorgeous, sweet daughter. "But we both know that's not true. Anyway, at least one of us will look beautiful."

"Mia's too young to get married," Kelly went on blithely. "I'm never getting married. Especially not to a dork like Carl Baker – I don't know what she sees in him."

Janine frowned. Privately, she agreed that nineteen was very young to take such a big step, but then Mia had always been mature for her age. She was a lovely girl, shy and sensible. She'd seen a lot her when she was younger, but they'd hardly spoken lately. Poor Mia was probably rushed off her feet with wedding plans.

"I expect she loves him," she told Kelly. That's the usual reason to get married, isn't it."

"Didn't help much with you and Dad, did it?"

Ouch, Janine thought, changing her mind about Kelly being gorgeous and sweet. Mentions of her ex-husband still hurt far more than she wanted to admit. She wasn't looking forward to seeing him at the wedding with his new girlfriend, who was thin – naturally.

Blimey, she was going to have to lose some weight before then. Perhaps she could get a padlock for the biscuit tin and the fridge, and she could have a ceremonial burning of all the take-away menus in the house.

They were on their way to school the next day when Kelly said hesitantly. "You could always try a slimming club. Sharon Tate's mum lost three stone at hers."

"Bet it took more than ten weeks," Janine muttered, slowing for a red light.

"Yes, but you don't need to lose three stone. A stone wouldn't take long, would it?"

"I'm not a slimming club type of person, though, darling. I can't think of anything worse than sitting in a room with a load of women discussing diets."

"It's not just women who go these days. There are three men in Sharon's Mum's group."

"That sounds even worse," Janine said, and then felt guilty at her daughter's pained expression. "All right, I'll think about it," she said, as they pulled up at the school gates. "Have a good day, pet."

She still wasn't quite sure how on earth she'd let herself be talked into it when she walked into the

Della Galton

"New You" Slimming Club the following Tuesday evening. As she stood at the end of a queue of chattering women she very nearly lost her nerve and ran. It was only the fact that she'd promised Kelly that stopped her. The class was being held at a primary school about two miles from where she lived, and there was a board at the entrance that said, 'Come on in, you have nothing to lose, but weight.'

She could think of a lot of other things she had to lose. Dignity being the main one. The last time she'd been to a slimming club, the group leader had thought it motivating to tell everyone in the room how much you weighed. Mind you, that had been several years ago. She closed her eyes and prayed things had changed.

Other Della Galton Novellas

Available now from amazon
and wherever you purchased this book:

Ten Weeks To Target
Genre: Romance

Shadowman
Genre: Cosy Crime / Thriller

Meltwater
Genre: Romance / Family

Della Galton

Ice And A Slice

ice and a slice

how many drinks does it take to erase the past?

Della Galton

THE THIRD FULL-LENGTH NOVEL FROM DELLA GALTON

The Wish List

Life should be idyllic, and it pretty much is for Sarah-Jane. Marriage to Tom is wonderful, even if he is hardly ever home. And lots of people have catastrophic fall-outs with their sister, don't they? They're bound to make it up some day. Just not right now, OK! And as for her drinking, yes it's true, she occasionally has one glass of wine too many, but everyone does that. It's hardly a massive problem, is it? Her best friend, Tanya, has much worse problems. Sarah-Jane's determined to help her out with them – just as soon as she's convinced Kit, the very nice man at the addiction clinic, that she's perfectly fine.

She is perfectly fine, isn't she?

Praise for Della's novels

"Della's writing is stylish, moving, original and fun : a wonderfully satisfying journey to a destination you can eagerly anticipate without ever guessing."
Liz Smith, Fiction Editor, My Weekly

**VISIT AMAZON TO
BUY THE BOOK
AND FIND OUT MORE DELLA'S FICTION AT
DELLAGALTON.CO.UK**

Della Galton

Other Della Galton Titles

Available now from amazon
and wherever you purchased this book:

**The Novel Writer's Toolshed
for Short Story Writers**
From soundhaven books, 2013
Genre: Non-Fiction

How to Eat Loads and Stay Slim
by Della Galton & Peter Jones
From soundhaven books, 2013
Genre: Non-Fiction

The Short Story Writer's Toolshed
From soundhaven books, 2012
Genre: Non-Fiction

More Della Galton Titles

The Dog with Nine Lives
From Accent Press, 2010
Genre: Fiction

Helter Skelter
From Accent Press, 2007
Genre: Fiction

Passing Shadows
From Accent Press, 2006
Genre: Fiction

For a complete list of titles from
soundhaven books
visit
www.soundhaven.com

Made in the USA
Charleston, SC
22 August 2014